My name is Sam Harding. I was born in 1810 in southwestern Indiana near the small town of Little Pigeon Creek. My parents, James and Martha, raised my two younger sisters and me in a small, attractive log cabin that my father built on fifty acres of beautiful farmland.

On our farm we grew corn and wheat. We even grew some cotton and tobacco. There were also horses, cows, chickens, and a couple dogs running around the farm. Our father put food in our bellies and sometimes, when we were good, a little money in our pockets. We were poor, but we didn't feel poor. Mama always said, "We have each other, and that's all that matters."

To Abraham Lincoln, who proved that a common touch and
the desire to make a difference in the world can overcome
all obstacles and lead to greatness.

Acknowledgment
I would like to thank Thomas B. Schad for editing my book.

Publishers Cataloging-in-Publication Data

Bloch, Robert L.

   My best friend, Abe Lincoln : a tale of two boys from Indiana / by
Robert L. Bloch ; illustrations by John W. Ewing. p. cm.

   Summary: Based on historical details, this is a fictional account of
the special bond between Abraham Lincoln and his closest childhood
friend.
   ISBN-9781466373839
   [1. Lincoln, Abraham, 1809-1865—Childhood and youth—Juvenile
fiction. 2. Best friends—Juvenile fiction. 3. Friendship—Juvenile
fiction.] I. Ewing, John W., ill. II. Title.   2010937873

115 Bluebill Drive
Savannah, GA 31419
United States
(888) 300-1961

This book was published with the assistance of the helpful folks at DragonPencil.com

CPSIA facility code: BP 304917

As I grew older, my mother thought it was important for me to get an education. When I was ten years old, I attended my first day of class in a small one-room cabin they called a "blab school." Children would "blab" each lesson out loud and repeat it over and over again until they knew it by heart.

In our classroom, we had about a dozen children ranging in age from six to twelve years old. I was one of the older children, along with an eleven-year-old boy who moved to Little Pigeon Creek from Kentucky. His name was Abe Lincoln. We instantly became best friends.

Abe was at least a head taller than the other boys in class and was so skinny that he looked like a walking skeleton. He was so tall and grew so fast that his pants were always too short. Abe was a sight to see!

Abe was a great student and had an amazing memory. Once he got hold of a new word or thought, he never forgot it. I think he was just about as smart as our teacher.

Every chance we got, we went fishing at the creek our town was named after, Little Pigeon Creek. An old Kickapoo Indian tribe lived on the hill just above the deep, winding waters. They were extremely proud and friendly people.

Abe and I enjoyed playing with the children of the tribe. Sometimes we liked to pretend we were brave Indian warriors. It was fun dressing up in their beaded clothing and moccasins and playing with their bows and arrows.

I remember one warm summer day when Abe and I explored a dark cave with a couple of our Indian friends. We yelled into the cave to hear the echo of our voices. Then, all of a sudden, several bats flew out of the cave toward us! We were so scared that we ran as fast as we could all the way home.

Abe learned at an early age how to entertain an audience with his folksy humor. On Sunday morning at church, he would watch the preacher give the sermon. Afterwards, he would gather our friends around him, stand on a tree stump, and tell us a funny story. He was such an amazing orator that none of us would move a muscle as he spoke. Everyone loved his high-pitched laughter.

Abe also had a talent for expressing his thoughts and ideas. "Someday Abe will make an excellent lawyer," my father said, "or maybe even a politician!"

Abe could be very serious and was a hard worker. Sometimes I would not see my friend for days and days. But I always knew what he was doing: reading, studying, working in the fields with his dad, and then more reading. Even though Abe attended school, he was mostly self-taught.

Abe read every book he could lay his hands on. He would walk miles just to borrow a book from friends and neighbors. Through reading, Abe met heroes like George Washington and Thomas Jefferson, people who made a big difference in our country.

Abe was not very close to his father. Thomas didn't understand why his son preferred reading over working on the farm. Abe adored his stepmother, Sally. She always treated Abe and his sister, Sarah, like her own. The children lovingly called her "mother," even though their real mother died only a few years before. Although Sally couldn't read or write, she encouraged Abe's love of learning.

I spent many memorable nights at the Lincoln cabin with Abe. We always had a warm, tasty supper with great conversation around the table. Dessert was the best part! Sally served delicious apple dumplings made from an old Lincoln family recipe. After dinner the two of us would go outside and play hide and seek. Abe was so big and tall he was always easy to find.

One day my family traveled to nearby Owensboro, Kentucky, to visit our relatives. Abe came with us. We were surprised to see a slave market in the center of town. Slaves were sold to whoever offered the most money. Families were often separated, never to see their loved ones again.

Abe and I couldn't stop thinking about slavery. It made us very angry and upset. "No one should be allowed to buy another person," fumed Abe, "or force him to work without pay."

Life in the early 1800's was very difficult. My father worked hard but just couldn't make ends meet in Indiana. So, in 1823, we had to sell our farm and move east to Dayton, Ohio.

I'll never forget the day I had to say goodbye to my best friend, Abe. "Do you think we'll ever see each other again?" I asked him.

"I sure hope so," he replied, his voice cracking. But that was the very last time I saw Abe Lincoln.

Just before we moved, Abe and I gave each other gifts. I gave him a nice, large arrowhead that I found near the creek. He gave me a wonderful book called *Robinson Crusoe* by Daniel Defoe. It was even signed by Abe. After all these years, I still have that book.

forth upon this continent, a new nation, concei
can never forget what they did here. It is for

For thirty-five years I didn't hear a thing about Abe, but I never forgot him. Then, in 1858, I read about the Lincoln - Douglas slavery debates that took place in Illinois. Abe argued that slavery was wrong and should not be allowed to spread to any new states. I told my wife with a big grin, "That is the same Abe Lincoln that I knew many years ago."

These debates made him famous throughout the country. The next thing I knew, Abraham Lincoln was the sixteenth President of the United States! I proudly voted for him. My childhood friend from Indiana now had the most important job in America. I never dreamed this would happen, but I bet he did. Abe always dreamed big.

President Lincoln led the Northern states to victory over the Southern states in our long and bloody Civil War. He brought the country together for the first time in its history by ending slavery.

Abe healed our nation's spirit and is remembered as one of our greatest Presidents. I am very proud that Abe Lincoln was my best friend and I was his. He proved that if you study hard, work hard, and treat everyone with respect, you can be anything you want to be in life.

Most people knew him as President Lincoln. I just knew him as the tall, skinny boy from Kentucky who I used to play Indian with and go fishing with on bright sunny days. My memories of my life with Abe will be with me always.

~Sam Harding   March 1882

The Author

Robert Bloch has worked at the H&R Block Foundation since 1989. He lives in Mission Hills, Kansas, and has four sons and a wonderful wife. Bob graduated from Menlo College in Menlo Park, California (1974) and the University of Missouri at Kansas City (1979). His passions are Art History and American History.

Bob's great-great-grandfather, Jonas Wollman, was one of fifty-two Leavenworth merchants and businessmen who signed a letter written by Mark Delahay requesting that Abraham Lincoln visit Leavenworth, Kansas. Lincoln obliged by traveling there to give his first campaign speech in December, 1859.

The Illustrator

John Ewing joined the team at Walt Disney Studios in Burbank, where he helped craft classic feature films, including *Sleeping Beauty*, *The Sword in the Stone*, *The Jungle Book*, *Winnie the Pooh*, and 1961's Oscar-nominated *Aquamania*. After Disney, Ewing went to New Zealand and launched Freelance Animators Ltd., carrying out contract work for Disney and Warner Bros. In recent years, he has stepped back from the school to spend more time on his interests, flying small aircraft and illustrating children's books. He is also the author and illustrator of *The Cessna, The Sky, ...and the Cartoonist*. John lives in New Zealand and can be visited online at www.DragonPencil.com.